DOCKSIDE

STAGE 3

BOOK 5

BAD MOOD

John Townsend

RISING STARS

You look like you're in a good mood, Rich.

Yeah, I've just had a text from my boss. He wants me to work all next week. I need the cash.

Just a bit of food each day. I'll pay you.
Notification
Contacts
He also wants me to feed his cat when he's away.

That's good news.

Yes, but I'm fed up at home. I'm so cross with JJ. He stole my new T-shirt and got blue ink on it.

Oops!
Notification
Contacts

Then his pet snake got out and hid in my shoe.
Notification
Contacts
No!

It‘s true, Lexi.
What did JJ say?

He never knew. He still hasn't got a clue. So I'll tell him now. I'll send a text.

I'm in a bad mood. I'm mad with you and your stupid pet. Stay out of my way. Rich
Notification

I've just sent it … ooh!

What's up, Rich?

I sent it to my boss!